For Mom and Dad,
with memories of Tehachapi

First edition 2004

Library of Congress Cataloging-in-Publication Data
Pedersen, Janet. • Millie wants to play! / Janet Pedersen.
p.   cm.
Summary: Millie the cow is awake early in the morning but waits until
she hears the other animals making noise before she joins them in play.
ISBN 0-7636-1993-0
[1. Animal sounds—Fiction. 2. Cows—Fiction.
3. Domestic animals—Fiction. 4. Morning—Fiction.]
PZ7.P43233 Mi 2004
[E]—dc21   2002067665

2 4 6 8 10 9 7 5 3 1

Printed in China
This book was typeset in Gararond Medium.
The illustrations were done in gouache,
watercolor, crayon, and pen.

Candlewick Press
2067 Massachusetts Avenue
Cambridge, Massachusetts 02140

visit us at www.candlewick.com

Millie Wants to Play!

Janet Pedersen

CANDLEWICK PRESS
CAMBRIDGE, MASSACHUSETTS

The barnyard was quiet
and calm.

Millie opened her eyes.
Everyone is still asleep and I'm
ready to play! Millie thought.

But Millie had to wait. She had to
wait for the loud rise-and-shine sound
that meant time to play!

Just then, Millie heard

Baaaa!
   Ba-a-a-a!
Baaaa!

That's not the rise-and-shine
sound, Millie thought.
Too low and ripply.
That sounds like…

Lamb!

Lamb baaed and
shook his woolly coat.
But the others were still asleep,
so Millie waited.

Then Millie heard

Oink.
Snuffle.
Oink.
Oink!

That's not the rise-and-shine
sound, Millie thought.
Too deep and snorty.
Sounds like...

Pig!

Pig oinked and wiggled her snout in a greeting.
Millie swished her tail, but waited.

Then Millie heard

Neigh!
Ne-e-e-e-eigh!
NEIGH!

That's not the rise-and-shine
sound, Millie thought.
Too high and giggly.
Sounds like…

Pony!

Pony neighed and nodded good morning.
Millie swished her tail and stamped
her hooves, but still she waited.

At last Millie heard a sound
as loud as a trumpet.
It was the sound
she'd been waiting for.

Cock-a-doodle doooooo!

The rise-and-shine sound!
thought Millie.
Sounds like…

Rooster!

The barnyard woke with sound as Rooster crowed and flapped his wings.

Millie shook her ears,
swished her tail,
and stamped her hooves.
She could wait no longer....

oooooo!

Time to play!